Pecos Bill and Slue-Foot Sue

Stephanie Herweck Paris

Assistant Editor
Leslie Huber, M.A.

Editorial Director
Dona Herweck Rice

Editor-in-Chief
Sharon Coan, M.S.Ed.

Editorial Manager
Gisela Lee, M.A.

Creative Director
Lee Aucoin

Illustration Manager/Designer
Timothy J. Bradley

Cover Art and Illustration
Agi Palinay

Publisher
Rachelle Cracchiolo, M.S.Ed.

Teacher Created Materials
5301 Oceanus Drive
Huntington Beach, CA 92649-1030
http://www.tcmpub.com

ISBN 978-1-4333-0991-5

Pecos Bill and Slue-Foot Sue

Story Summary

Pecos Bill was the rootinest, tootinest, ripsnortinest cowboy of all time. He invented bronco busting, and he could shoot straighter and ride faster than any cowpoke before or after him. Raised by coyotes, Bill learned early how to cope with just about anything. But, what would happen when Bill was suddenly faced with a horse named Widowmaker and a woman who could ride a catfish? Had our hero met his match? Read the story and find out!

Tips for Performing Reader's Theater

Adapted from Aaron Shepard

- Don't let your script hide your face. If you can't see the audience, your script is too high.
- Look up often when you speak. Don't just look at your script.
- Talk slowly so the audience knows what you are saying.
- Talk loudly so everyone can hear you.
- Talk with feelings. If the character is sad, let your voice be sad. If the character is surprised, let your voice be surprised.
- Stand up straight. Keep your hands and feet still.
- Remember that even when you are not talking, you are still your character.
- Narrator, be sure to give the characters enough time for their lines.

Tips for Performing Reader's Theater *(cont.)*

- If the audience laughs, wait for them to stop before you speak again.
- If someone in the audience talks, don't pay attention.
- If someone walks into the room, don't pay attention.
- If you make a mistake, pretend it was right.
- If you drop something, try to leave it where it is until the audience is looking somewhere else.
- If a reader forgets to read his or her part, see if you can read the part instead, make something up, or just skip over it. Don't whisper to the reader!
- If a reader falls down during the performance, pretend it didn't happen.

Pecos Bill and Slue-Foot Sue

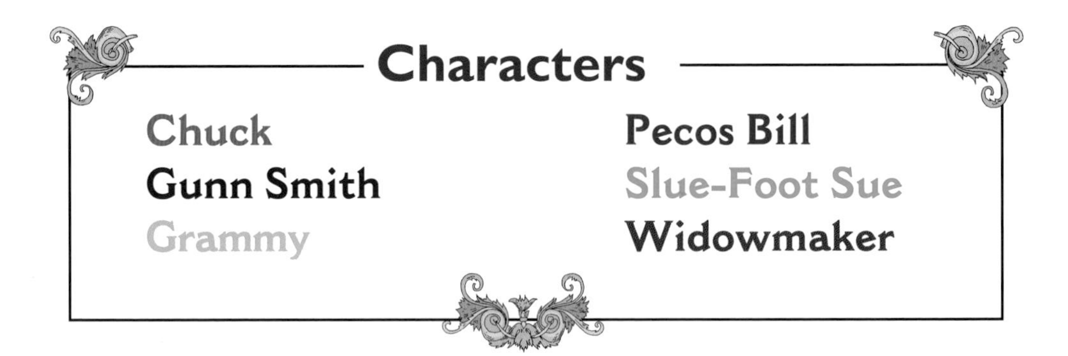

Characters

Chuck
Gunn Smith
Grammy
Pecos Bill
Slue-Foot Sue
Widowmaker

Setting

This reader's theater takes place on the open plains in the great state of Texas, sometime in the 1800s.

Act I

Slue-Foot Sue: Yooohooo! Neighbors! Anybody home?

Chuck: Well, howdy ma'am! Did I hear you say *neighbor*? Are you new in these parts?

Slue-Foot Sue: Ma'am? I don't stand much on formalities. I can ride any critter big enough to hold me and shoot twice as well as any man I have ever met. They call me Slue-Foot Sue, and I just moved into that ranch over yonder.

Chuck: Pleased to meet you, Slue-Foot Sue. My name is Bob, but most folks call me Chuck, because whenever we're in camp, I like to hang around the chuck wagon and grab myself a snack! My friend here is named . . . well, I can't properly pronounce her name, because I don't speak Coyote. She is old and wise, so we call her Grammy as a sign of respect.

Grammy: Pleased to meet you, Human Sue.

Slue-Foot Sue: The pleasure is all mine, Grammy. You two have got my curiosity up, though. A coyote and a cowboy sitting out here like peas in a pod? Now, there has to be a good story in that!

Grammy: It is a very good story, indeed, but it is not our own. It is the story of Pecos Bill.

Slue-Foot Sue: Pecos Bill? Well, I am always up for an interesting tale. Would you consider recounting it for me?

Chuck: Of course! There once was a family with many children. In fact, there were 18 in all, each more active than the last. And the youngest one was named Bill.

Grammy: I think the family must have been part coyote, because as soon as a neighbor moved in 50 miles away, they got to feeling itchy, like someone was looking over their shoulder. So, they decided to pack up and leave.

Chuck: Bill's family traveled west in an old covered wagon. The children would sit in the back and make so much noise that their Ma and Pa couldn't hear thunder rolling! Everyone could tell that Bill was special even then. He used a bowie knife for a teething ring, and when they were in the wild, he would hop out of the wagon and find grizzly cubs to wrestle.

Grammy: One day, when Bill was about four years old, the wagon hit a rock as the family was crossing the Pecos River in Texas. Bill flew out the back and landed in the water! With so many pups making so much noise, it was a while before anyone noticed that he was gone.

Slue-Foot Sue: Jumpin' Jehosaphat, how did he ever survive that?

Chuck: He taught himself to swim along the way! But the current was too swift, and there was no getting back. The family often thought about Bill. Since he was lost along the Pecos River, they took to calling him Pecos Bill.

Grammy: I found him: a wet, furless pup sitting by the side of the river. At first, I was wary. I had heard of strange creatures called human beings. I kept my guard.

Slue-Foot Sue: No one could blame you for that!

Chuck: Grammy did what any clear-thinking coyote would do. She hopped back and forth, testing Bill, coyote-style, to see if he was friend or foe. Bill did the logical thing. He gave her a big hug! Then he scratched her behind the ears!

Grammy: I knew then that this pup was meant to be a coyote! As leader of Coyote Pack 494, I resolved to adopt and raise him. Bill grew strong and learned the laws of the wild. We taught him to hunt, to howl at the moon, and to avoid being seen when you don't want to be seen.

Chuck: Lucky for me, Bill was not that interested in that last lesson! One day, I came across the wildest-looking man I had ever seen. I asked him what sort of man he might be.

Grammy:	Bill replied that he was not a mangy human! He was an honorable, brave coyote!
Chuck:	He was lean and tan and had the most disorderly beard you could imagine. But, there was something too familiar about him to ignore. I decided to make him my friend.
Grammy:	Now, the pack tried to give Bill every advantage of coyote life. But, there was one thing we could not provide him.
Chuck:	Well, I noticed it right away. "Friend," I said, "there is something every coyote has got, and you certainly do not: a beautiful bushy tail!"
Grammy:	Bill was horrified. He had never looked before, but he did then. Sure enough, no tail! He was human after all. Bill resolved to go with Chuck to learn the ways of the humans. But the pack never abandoned him!
Chuck:	I took Bill down to the river and got him cleaned up. Once we got him shaved, my eyes popped. He was the spittin' image of Pa! This wild man was my own long-lost brother, Pecos Bill!

Act 2

Pecos Bill: Well, of course I'm your brother, Chuck! Who else would I be? Whoa. You have company.

Gunn Smith: Hello, Chuck. Hello, Grammy. We were just checking on the herd. Care to introduce us to your friend?

Chuck: Miss Sue, may I present Gunn Smith and my brother, Pecos Bill.

Slue-Foot Sue: Howdy, fellers! I am your new neighbor on the west side.

Pecos Bill: I'm right pleased to make your acquaintance, Miss Sue!

Slue-Foot Sue: I'm pleased to meet you, too, Bill! Chuck and Grammy here were just telling me a few stories about how you all met up. But, we hadn't gotten to your part, Gunn Smith.

Gunn Smith: Ah, well now, how I met Bill? That is a mighty fine story! It all began with Bill deciding one day to take a ride.

Pecos Bill: Yes, my horse tripped on a stone and came up lame. We were miles from camp, so I did the reasonable thing. I picked that horse up and started running for home!

Grammy: Now, the King of the Rattlers is a 40-foot serpent with fangs the size of two jackknifes. That day, he was lying in wait for the first creature he saw. When he saw Bill and the horse, he thought he had gotten doubly lucky because he could get two meals in one!

Pecos Bill: That viper wrapped its coils around me. We wrestled a day and a night, with his fangs inching toward my face and my hands around his throat! It was a real toss-up!

Chuck: My brother is being modest. He whooped that snake up and down the mesa until every last drop of venom was squeezed out and it was as skinny as a bullwhip!

Gunn Smith: Then, he wrapped that snake around his arm, picked up his lame horse, and started trotting back toward camp!

Grammy: The next creature Bill came across was a wild cougar. Now, cougars can be sweet and gentle with their friends. But if you catch one hungry or in a mood, watch out! This one was both hungry *and* in a mood!

Chuck: She was also big! Thinking that Bill and his horse would fill up her tummy, she leaped on Bill from behind.

Gunn Smith: Quick as a whistle, Bill grabbed that snake from his arm and wrapped it around the cougar's neck. Then, he hopped on her back and rode her through the canyon!

Chuck: She pounced and bucked, but Bill never let go. After three days and nights, she finally collapsed and became as tame as a pony. Bill had invented Bronco Busting!

Poem: I Want to Be a Cowboy

Grammy: Once again, Bill picked up his horse, wrapped his snake-whip around his arm, climbed onto the cougar, and started for home.

Gunn Smith: Only, he happened upon the camp of the meanest band of outlaws ever to roam the plains: the Devil's Gate Gang.

Pecos Bill: Well, I had some ideas about how to make those fellers useful, so when I got close, I called out loud and clear, "Who is in charge of this here camp?"

Chuck: The biggest, toughest-looking cowboy of 'em all stood up and walked over. He had black hair, black whiskers, and a scar that ran down his face from top to bottom.

Slue-Foot Sue: Why, Gunn Smith, you fit that description!

Gunn Smith: Right you are, Miss Sue. That was me. I walked up and looked Bill over. I looked at the snake, the cougar, and the horse that Bill was carrying. Then, I spoke as clearly as he had. "Stranger," I said, "I *was* in charge, but you are now!"

Pecos Bill: That is when I put the Devil's Gate Gang in the business of cattle ranching!

Chuck: Heh, I never tire of hearing that story! So, Gunn Smith, what news do you have on the herd?

Gunn Smith: Well, the boss and I were just talking about something. Bill, I'm not sure how to put this, but . . . well, that cougar of yours frightens the herd. The gang wants you to get a different mount when you are working the cattle.

Song: Git Along Little Dogies

Slue-Foot Sue: You know, I just came from town, where I overheard some fellers talking. They had just spotted Widowmaker up on the ridge. They said, "No human alive can ride him, unless maybe it's Pecos Bill!" At the time, I didn't know what they meant, but I do now. If you leave right away, you might be able to catch up with him.

Pecos Bill: Is that so? Well, Miss Sue, if you think it's the right thing to do, then I will leave right away!

Grammy: And so, Pecos Bill set off to find the horse known as Widowmaker.

Act 3

Widowmaker: Uh-oh! Here comes another one of those pesky two-legs! They are always annoying me! You would think that after I bucked off a hundred of 'em, they would stop trying!

Pecos Bill: Ho there, friend, wait up a while. I want to talk with you!

Widowmaker: Talk with me? Well, that's different! There is something strange about this two-leg. He moves like one of my four-legged brothers. He almost lopes like a coyote!

Pecos Bill: Greetings, friend. Fine morning, isn't it?

Widowmaker: It is a beautiful day! There is dew on the grass and . . . wait! You speak horse?

Pecos Bill: My Grammy taught me, long ago.

Widowmaker: Well, greetings to you, human. You are polite. But I am afraid you have wasted the trip out here.

Pecos Bill: Thank you kindly, but why do you say so?

Widowmaker: Well, unless I am mistaken, you have come here to ride me, and that just isn't going to happen. I can buck any human, and I won't be ridden by a human I can buck!

Pecos Bill: Oh, is that the problem, then? Would you mind if I give it a try? I always hanker for a good challenge.

Widowmaker: Be my guest, but it hardly seems worth the trouble.

Grammy: With that, Pecos Bill tossed his snake-lariat around Widowmaker's neck and swung up on the horse's back.

Gunn Smith: Widowmaker began to kick up his heels. He bucked and he jumped, but Bill held on tight!

Pecos Bill: Ha! This is terrific! Please continue!

Widowmaker: If you insist!

Gunn Smith: Widowmaker kicked and leaped and bucked higher, but Bill held on. Anyone watching would have to say that the two of them were having fun!

Chuck: Pretty soon, Widowmaker was leaping as high as the hills. But Bill just held on and laughed.

Grammy: For seven whole days, Bill and Widowmaker leaped and bucked and twirled around the Texas range, neither one getting tired and neither one willing to give up. Then, suddenly, Widowmaker simply stopped.

Pecos Bill: I hope you didn't stop on my account!

Widowmaker: That was fun, but I am getting hungry. And, besides, I reckon that if you can hold on for seven days, maybe you are the rider for me. If I go with you, will you feed me oats?

Pecos Bill: Oats? I will feed you dynamite if you want it, friend.

Widowmaker: Perfect! But there is one more thing. I don't like the name Widowmaker. My friends call me Lightning.

Pecos Bill: Then, Lightning, how would you like to come back and meet the rest of my crew?

Widowmaker: That would suit me just fine. Want a ride back to camp?

Act 4

Gunn Smith: Howdy, Bill! Wowee! Is that Widowmaker you're riding?

Pecos Bill: His name is Lightning now. Have you seen Miss Sue?

Gunn Smith: Last I saw, she was headed down to the river.

Widowmaker: What is so special about this Sue person?

Pecos Bill: The second you meet her, you will understand.

Grammy: But when Bill got to the river, his jaw nearly unhinged! Sue was riding on a catfish the size of a small elephant!

Pecos Bill: Miss Sue, is that you?

Slue-Foot Sue: It's me, all right! Do you like my noble steed?

Pecos Bill: Wow, Miss Sue, I don't know what to say. I came here to show off my new mount. Slue-Foot Sue, please meet Lightning, previously known as Widowmaker!

Slue-Foot Sue: Lightning! Well, doesn't that beat all. Mister Pecos Bill, it looks to me like we may have some things in common.

Pecos Bill: Miss Sue, you are the only lady for me. Would you do me the honor of becoming my bride?

Slue-Foot Sue: Oh, Bill, nothing would make me happier. Only, I always wanted to wear a big fancy dress with one of those newfangled steel-spring bustles to my wedding.

Pecos Bill: Absolutely, my love, consider it done.

Slue-Foot Sue: And, well, I hate to mention it, but I can't exactly ride home from my wedding on a fish! May I ride Widowma . . . excuse me, Lightning, on the way to our honeymoon?

Pecos Bill: Anything you want, my darling! I will get the dress and arrange for a preacher!

Widowmaker: Now, either one of these wonderful people could have consulted me about this plan, but nobody did.

Act 5

Gunn Smith: Bill and Sue met early the next day, with their friends and family gathered, to join in holy matrimony.

Chuck: It was a beautiful ceremony, and the bride was lovely.

Grammy: They said their "I do's" and sealed the matter with a heartfelt kiss, human-style. Sue was so eager to get going that she turned and made a bound onto Lightning's back!

Widowmaker: She startled me so! I couldn't help it. I gave one great kick. Up, up, up she flew! Up past the mountain! Up past the clouds! Up she went until her hair brushed the moon!

Gunn Smith: Then she came down! Down through the clouds, down past the hills, down to the ground, and she landed, sproing, right on that steel-spring bustle!

Grammy: Back up she flew, higher and higher. Again she touched the moon. Then down, down she came, back onto that springy bustle.

Slue-Foot Sue: BIIIILLLLL!!! CCCAAATTCCHH MEEEE!

Pecos Bill: Hold on, Sue! I will save you!

Chuck: And poor Bill did try! He chased Slue-Foot Sue all over Texas. But no matter where he was, Sue was always just ahead. The poor groom watched his bride bounce between the Earth and the moon again and again.

Gunn Smith: Bill began to despair. He didn't know what to do.

Grammy: Just then he noticed a passing tornado! As quick as Lightning could get him there, Bill chased after that twister and lassoed it!

Pecos Bill: Hang on, honey! I am coming for you!

Slue-Foot Sue: USSSEEE TTTTHHEE RRROOPPPEEE!

Widowmaker: Bill swung himself up on that tornado and made his lariat ready. Just as Sue passed by, Bill caught his wonderful bride!

Slue-Foot Sue: Oh, Bill, I knew you could do it!

Pecos Bill: Oh, Sue, if anything bad ever happened to you, I could never forgive myself!

Gunn Smith: Slue-Foot Sue and Bill rode that twister down past Texas, past New Mexico, past Arizona, and finally landed with a plop right onto a wagon train in the middle of California.

Chuck: Who do you think it was but our ma and pa and 16 of our brothers and sisters! They were still looking for a place that had a little elbowroom!

Gunn Smith: Bill and Slue-Foot Sue invited the whole clan back to their spread in Texas. Bill said that there wasn't a roomier place on earth. Slue-Foot Sue said there wasn't even a roomier place on the moon!

Grammy: So, all of Bill's family came back to Texas and put down roots deeper than a wild fig tree. And it is said that if they haven't moved on, they are living there happily, still.

I Want to Be a Cowboy

Traditional

I want to be a cowboy and with the cowboys stand,
Big spurs upon my boot heels and a lasso in my hand;
My hat broad-brimmed and belted upon my head I'll place,
And wear my *chaparajos* with elegance and grace.

The first bright beam of sunlight that paints the east with red
Would call forth to breakfast on bacon, beans, and bread;
And then upon my bronco, so festive and so bold,
I'd rope the frisky heifer and chase the three-year-old.

Git Along Little Dogies

Cowboy Traditional

As I walked out one morning for pleasure,
I spied a young cowpuncher riding along;
His hat was throwed back and his spurs were a-jingling,
And as he approached he was singin' this song.

Chorus:
Woopie ti yi yo, git along little dogies,
It's your misfortune and none of my own.
Woopie ti yi yo, git along little dogies,
For you know that Wyoming will be your new home.

Early in springtime we round up the dogies,
Mark 'em and brand 'em and bob off their tails,
Round up our horses, load up the chuck wagons,
And then throw the dogies out onto the trail.

Chorus

Glossary

bowie knife—a thick, single-edged hunting knife

bronco—an unbroken or wild horse

bustle—the framework for holding draped fabric over the back end of women's skirts

chaparajos—Spanish for *chaps*, a sturdy leg covering

chuck wagon—wagon holding cooking supplies and food

dogie—a cow, or sometimes more specifically, a motherless calf

foe—an enemy

formalities—social rules

hanker—to yearn or desire

jackknifes—large pocketknifes

Jumpin' Jehosaphat—mild oath

lame—unable to walk properly because of injury or disability

lariat—a long, light rope used for catching livestock

lasso—to catch, using a thrown loop of rope

lopes—moves in an easy, natural way

mangy—shabby, worn, or afflicted with a skin disease

mesa—a raised, flat area of land

venom—poison

viper—a kind of poisonous snake